Pear Under the Stairs

ReadZone Books Limited

First published in this edition 2015

© in this edition ReadZone Books Limited 2015
© in text Christine Moorcroft 2010
© in illustrations Lisa Williams 2010

Christine Moorcroft has asserted her right under the Copyright Designs and Patents Act 1988 to be identified as the author of this work.

Lisa Williams has asserted her right under the Copyright Designs and Patents Act 1988 to be identified as the illustrator of this work.

Every attempt has been made by the Publisher to secure appropriate permissions for material reproduced in this book. If there has been any oversight we will be happy to rectify the situation in future editions or reprints. Written submissions should be made to the Publisher.

British Library Cataloguing in Publication Data (CIP) is available for this title.

Printed in Malta by Melita Press.

ISBN 978 1 78322 137 0

Visit our website: www.readzonebooks.com

Pear Under the Stairs

Christine Moorcroft
and Lisa Williams

READZONE

Clare Macnair
had a rare
pink
pear.

6

She didn't want to share
the pear,
so she hid it under
the stairs.

Then she heard a noise
somewhere.
She looked out
into the square.

A crowd was there
on the way to the fair.

"Have you a pear to spare?" called a man with green hair riding bareback on a mare.

13

14

What a scare!
It made Clare's hair
stand up in the air.

"Look!" she said.
"My pockets are bare.
There is no pear."

18

Then another, riding a bear,
stared at Clare and said,
"Don't you dare
hide that pear
under the stairs!"

He dashed onto the kerb
with a swoop and a swerve.
"Get off there!" called
Clare. "What a nerve!"

21

"This isn't fair.
You must learn to share.
We're coming in there
to get that pear!"

24

Clare stood on a chair and shouted, "Do what you like. I don't care.
You shall not have my pear."

The crowd stared.
Clare was not scared!

She slammed the door and
sped under the stairs.
What on earth was she doing
in there?

Out came Clare. She threw
the core without a care.
"There's your share of the
pear!"

Did you enjoy this book?

Look out for more *Redstart* titles –
first rhyming stories for beginning readers